Halloween

ABDO
Publishing Company

A Buddy Book
by
Julie Murray

Visit us at
www.abdopub.com

Published by Buddy Books, an imprint of ABDO Publishing Company, 4940 Viking Drive, Suite 622, Edina, Minnesota 55435. Copyright © 2003 by Abdo Consulting Group, Inc. International copyrights reserved in all countries. No part of this book may be reproduced in any form without written permission from the publisher.

Printed in the United States.

Edited by: Christy DeVillier
Contributing Editors: Matt Ray, Michael P. Goecke
Graphic Design: Denise Esner
Image Research: Deborah Coldiron
Cover Photograph: Corbis
Interior Photographs: Comstock, Corbis, Image Ideas, Photodisc

Library of Congress Cataloging-in-Publication Data

Murray, Julie, 1969-
   Halloween/Julie Murray.
      p. cm. — (Holidays. Set 1)
   Includes bibliographical references and index.
   Contents: What is Halloween? — The history of Halloween — The Roman festival— How Halloween got its name — Symbols of Halloween — Jack-o-lanterns — Halloween costumes — Trick-or-treating — Halloween today.
   ISBN 1-57765-952-X
     1. Halloween—Juvenile literature. [1. Halloween. 2. Holidays.] I. Title.

GT4965 .M87 2003
394.2646—dc21

2002026098

Table of Contents

What Is Halloween? 4

How Halloween Began 6

Roman Festivals 8

The Halloween Name 10

Halloween Costumes 12

Trick-or-treating 16

Halloween Today........................20

Important Words 23

Web Sites 23

Index 24

What Is Halloween?

Halloween is about dressing up, trick-or-treating, and having fun. People in Canada, the United States, England, Ireland, Wales, and Scotland celebrate Halloween. This **holiday** is on October 31st each year.

Fall is a time for pumpkins, hayrides, and Halloween.

How Halloween Began

Halloween **customs** began with the **Celts**. They lived about 2,000 years ago. The Celts lived in England, Scotland, Ireland, and other European countries. They celebrated the festival of Samhain on the last day of summer. For the Celts, this day was October 31st.

The **Celts** believed that dead people had spirits. They thought these spirits came to Earth on October 31st. The Celts left food and gifts for the spirits. They also wore masks to hide from the bad spirits. The Celts did not want bad spirits to take their bodies. Some people burned big fires to scare them away.

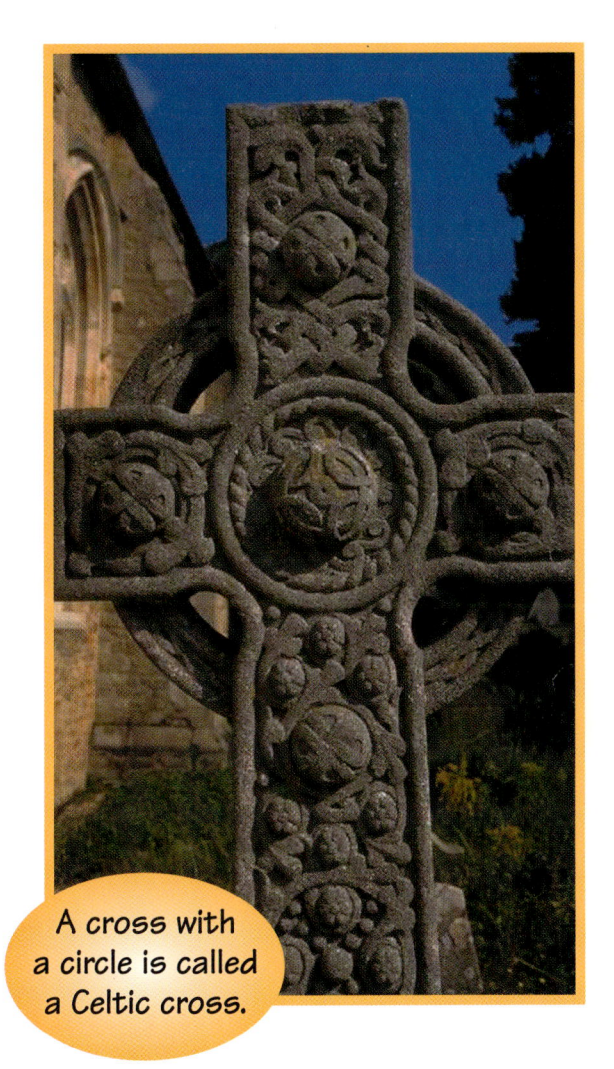

A cross with a circle is called a Celtic cross.

Roman Festivals

Hundreds of years later, the Romans took over the **Celt's** land. They began ruling the Celts. The Romans had their own festivals.

One Roman **holiday** was Feralia. It was a day to honor the dead.

The Romans also had a **harvest** festival in the fall. This was a fun festival that honored Pomona. Pomona was the Roman goddess of fruit trees. The Romans left apples and nuts for her.

Over time, the Romans and **Celts** began celebrating together. **Customs** from all of these festivals became Halloween.

An old Celtic church

The Halloween Name

The **Christians** did not like the **Celtic** and Roman festivals. They thought these **holidays** were unholy. The Christians set up their own holy day on November 1st. It was called All Saints' Day, or All Hallows. "Hallow" is another word for holy.

In Mexico, November 1st is a day to honor the souls of the dead.

The night before All Saints' Day was called All Hallows Eve. "Eve" means evening, or night. Over the years, All Hallows Eve changed to Halloween.

Halloween Costumes

The **Celtic custom** of wearing masks is still around today. People often wear **costumes** for Halloween.

Masks are common on Halloween.

Children often dress up for Halloween.

Some people wear scary **costumes**. They dress up to look like witches, ghosts, or vampires. Some people dress up like cartoon characters. Cowboy, clown, and princess costumes are common, too.

This person is dressed as a vampire.

14

Halloween Witches

Witches were real people who had their own beliefs. People began to think that witches were evil. They thought witches cast magic spells to harm others. But not all witches were harmful.

Halloween was a day for witches to gather. So, dressing up as a witch became a Halloween **custom**.

Trick-or-treating

Trick-or-treating is another Halloween **custom**. Children dress up in their **costumes**. Then, they go from house to house. They knock on doors and say, "Trick or treat!" People give trick-or-treaters candy and other goodies.

These children are dressed for trick-or-treating.

The trick-or-treating **custom** started in Europe. On Halloween in England, poor people knocked on doors. They begged for "soul cakes." These cakes were special bread treats. In return, the beggars prayed for the souls of the dead.

Today, candy is a common Halloween treat.

Another kind of trick-or-treating happened in Ireland. On Halloween, poor people went from house to house. They asked for money or food. These gifts were for Muck Olla. People believed Muck Olla punished those who did not give gifts. Giving gifts was safer than getting "tricked" by Muck Olla.

Jack-o'-lanterns

Making jack-o'-lanterns is a fun thing to do for Halloween. First, scoop out the inside of a pumpkin. Then, cut a scary or funny face into the outside of the pumpkin. Setting a light inside the pumpkin changes it into a jack-o'-lantern. The jack-o'-lantern **custom** came from Ireland.

Halloween Today

There are many fun ways to celebrate Halloween. Children enjoy dressing up and trick-or-treating. Halloween parties are fun, too. One Halloween game is bobbing for apples.

Bobbing for apples is a Halloween custom.

Not all Halloween costumes are scary.

Pumpkins taste good in Halloween pies and cookies.

Some people enjoy scaring themselves on Halloween. They tell each other spooky ghost stories. They go to special "haunted houses." But Halloween does not have to be scary. It is a fun **holiday** for children and adults.

Important Words

Celts people who lived about 2,000 years ago in many countries of western Europe.

Christians people who belong to a Christian religion. Christians follow the teachings of Jesus Christ.

costume clothes that people wear to look like someone or something else.

custom a practice that has been around a long time. Trick-or-treating is a Halloween custom.

harvest what is gathered from ripe crops. A harvest may be vegetables, fruits, or grains.

holiday a special time for celebration.

Web Sites

To learn more about Halloween,

visit ABDO Publishing Company on the World Wide Web. Web site links about Halloween are featured on our Book Links page. These links are routinely monitored and updated to provide the most current information available.

www.abdopub.com

Index

All Hallows **10**

All Hallows Eve **11**

All Saints' Day **10, 11**

Canada..........................**4**

Celts **6, 7, 8, 9, 10, 12**

Christians **10**

costumes **12, 14, 16, 21**

England **4, 6, 17**

Europe **6, 17**

Feralia..........................**8**

Ireland **4, 6, 18, 19**

jack-o'-lanterns **19**

masks **7, 12**

Muck Olla **18**

Pomona **8**

pumpkins............**5, 19, 22**

Romans **8, 9, 10**

Samhain **6**

Scotland **4, 6**

"soul cakes" **17**

trick-or-treating **4, 16, 17, 18, 20**

United States **4**

Wales **4**

witches...................**14, 15**